Holiday HA-HA'S

Valentine's Day
Jokes & Riddles

This book is dedicated with love to Clizia Gussoni.
—Craig Yoe

This book is dedicated with love to Craig Yoe.
—Clizia Gussoni

ISBN 0-8431-0482-1
A B C D E F G H I J

Holiday HA-HA'S

Valentine's Day
Jokes & Riddles

CRAIG YOE
Illustrated by Clizia Gussoni

LIBRARY O' LAUGHS

PSS!
PRICE STERN SLOAN

Candy hearts to: Jon Anderson, Kelli Chipponeri, AnnMarie Harris, Mara Conlon, Jayne Antipow, Joy Court, Rosalie Lent, and, of course, Clizia Gussoni.

Roses are red,
Violets are blue,
I wrote this joke book
just for you!

CRAIG

Craig Yoe

P.S. Though you look like a monkey
and you act like one, too!

What did the raindrop say on his wedding day?

-"I dew!"

What did one white bird say to the other white bird on Valentine's Day?

-"I dove you!"

What did one piece of bread say to the other piece of bread on Valentine's Day?

—"I loaf you!"

What did the pig give his girlfriend on Valentine's Day?

—An oink-le bracelet!

Teacher: Write your Valentine poem neater, please!

Student: If I write neater, you'll see how bad my spelling is!

Why was the bull afraid to ask someone on a date?

—Because he was a cow-ard!

Who lives with animals and makes people fall in love?

—Zoo-pid!

What flower is a candy?

—A lolli-poppy!

Why did the boy monkey give the girl monkey a Valentine?

—Because he was bananas for her!

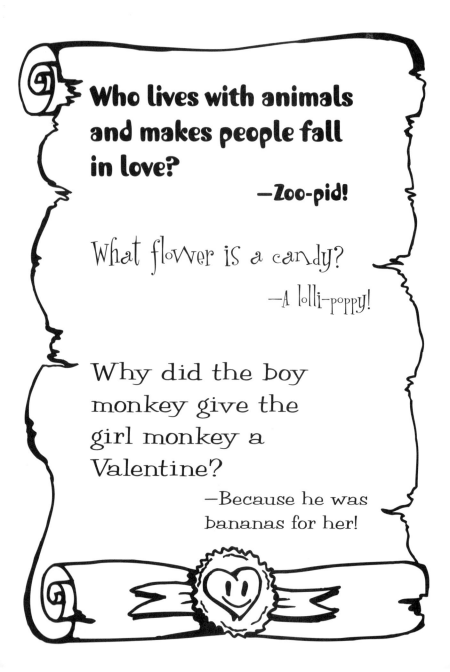

How do vegetables send love notes to each other on Valentine's Day?

-They use pea-mail!

What did the librarian give the kid with overdue books on February 14th?

-A Valen-fine!

I love you, moving van—you really move me!

I love you, librarian—our love is overdue!

I love you, plumber—you make me feel flush!

I love you, make-up artist—you make me blush!

WE'RE **BREAK** **ING** UP!

We're breaking up, fisherman-you gave me a line!

We're breaking up, Dracula-you have bat breath!

We're breaking up, banana-you gave me the slip!

We're breaking up, jump rope-you skipped out on me!

What do you get when you combine a computer with Juliet's boyfriend?

-ROM-eo!

What did one telephone give the other telephone on Valentine's Day?

-A ring!

Where do you put a donkey's Valentine?

—In his mule box!

Who did the zombie go out with on Valentine's Day?

—His ghoul-friend!

What did the mirror do when it got a funny Valentine?

—It cracked up!

What did the math book say to the geography book on Valentine's Day?

—"Atlas, our time has come!"

Why did the bicycles break up?

—They were tire-d of each other!

What should you say when someone tells you a joke on Valentine's Day?

-"Hearty-har-har!"

When do chickens hate Valentine's Day?

–When it falls on a Fry-day!

What did one bully say to the other bully on Valentine's Day?

–"I shove you!"

Why was the girl mad
on February 14th?

–Because her valentine
was choco-late!

Who did the bird marry on
Valentine's Day?

–His tweetheart!

What did one light say to the other light during a Valentine's Day blackout?

—"Wanna go out?"

What did one dirty shirt give the other dirty shirt on Valentine's Day?

—A ring around the collar!

What happened when the two 20-foot giants met?

—It was love at first height!

What did one rose say to the other rose on Valentine's Day?

—"You're my best bud!"

Why did the girl tailor get mad at the boy tailor?

-He bought her a sew-sew Valentine!

What does a bulldozer love to get on Valentine's Day?

—A doze-n roses!

They met on the
Internet–it was
love at first site!

What does a pig sign his Valentines
with?

—His pen!

What do bugs play at a
Valentine's Day party?

—Spin the beetle!

What is a rabbit's favorite song?

-"My Furry Valentine!"

Where does Superman's
Valentine live?

-On Lois Lane!

Why couldn't the jellyfish get up the nerve to ask the starfish on a date?

-Because he was spineless!

Why did the girl bird get mad at the boy bird?

—He bought her a cheep Valentine!

What does a greedy person hope to get on February 14th?

—A Valen-mine-mine-mine!

What does an average student say on Valentine's Day?

—"B Mine!"

What did one entryway say to the other entryway on Valentine's Day?

—"I a-door you!"

Did you hear that the glove and the cat got married on Valentine's Day?

—They wanted to have mittens!

What did the ladder give his girlfriend on Valentine's day?

—An engagement rung!

Who is green, leafy, eats bugs, and is the goddess of love?

-Venus Flytrap!

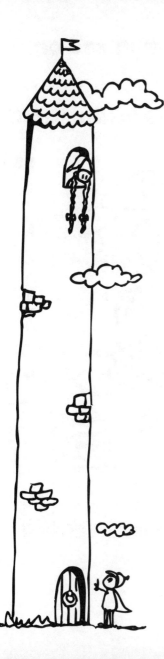

Why did the girl monster like the heart her boyfriend sent her on Valentine's Day?

-Because it was still beating!

Knock, knock!
  Who's there?
Ima!
  Ima who?
Ima funny
Valentine!

Why was the repairman sad on Valentine's Day?

—He had a broken heart!

Girl: I'm mad, you didn't send me a Valentine!
Boy: Yes I did!
Girl: Oh! What did it say?
Boy: "Merry Christmas!"

Why did the cows get married?

—Because they loved each udder!

What did one Vegetable give the other Vegetable on Valentine's Day?

—cauli-flowers!

Who did the bee take on a date on Valentine's Day?

—His honey!

I love you,
firefighter-you set
my heart ablaze!

I love you,
furnace-you make my
temperature rise!

I love you,
rabbit-you make
me hoppy!

I love you,
tailor-you put me on
pins and needles!

Who is the king of Valentine's Day?

-February the 14th!

What kind of ring did the rabbit give his girlfriend for Valentine's Day?

—One with 24 carrots!

What do librarians love to receive on Valentine's Day?

—Read roses!

What did the sheep say to his girlfriend on Valentine's Day?

—"I love ewe!"

What kind of music should you listen to on Valentine's Day?

-Pink rock!

How do fish send love notes to each other on Valentine's Day?

—They use sea-mail!

What did the ghost give his girlfriend on Valentine's Day?

—A boo-quet of flowers!

Why do golfers love Valentine's Day?

—Because it falls on February four-tee-nth!

I love you, vegetable—you carrot for me!

Why did the boy squirrel give the girl squirrel a Valentine?

—He was nuts for her!

Where do bunnies like to go on dates?

—To the sock hop!

What does a musician play for his love?

-Valen-tunes!

What did the astronomer say to his girlfriend?

-"I've got my sights set on you!"

What happened when the cookie got dumped on Valentine's Day?

–It felt crummy!

What flower lives at the North Pole?

—A f-rose!

Why can't Santa's helpers get dates on Valentine's Day?

–Because they're too s-elf-ish!

Craig: Did you know the window fell in love with the pane?

Clizia: Yes, love is blind!

Why did the rowboats break up?

—They drifted apart!

What does a bride send on February 14th?

—A Veil-intine!

What did the fisherman give the fish on February 14th?

—A Valen-line!

How do single cats meet each other?

—In the purr-sonals!

Why can't crabs get dates on Valentine's Day?

-Because they're too shellfish!

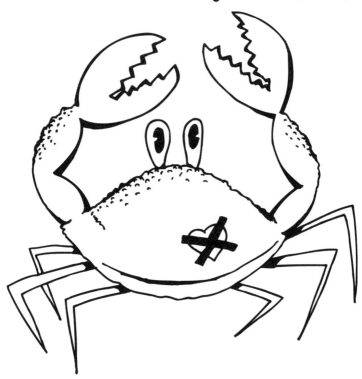

What do guys say to their sweethearts on February 14th?

-"Be my gal-entine!"

What did one runner say to the other runner on Valentine's Day?

—"I find you a-track-tive!"

Why does a storm love Valentine's Day?

—Because it's in Fe-brew-ary!

What's a Valentine's favorite musical instrument?

-The heart-sichord!

Where does a boat buy his Valentine cards?

-At the Hull-mark store!

What did one Valentine say to the other?

—"I love you whole-heartedly!"

They met in the park on a windy day—it was love at first kite!

What did the number 8 give the number 1 on February 14th?

—A Valen-nine!

Why do you find a lot of Valentines in a library?

-Because they're, well, red!

Who did the witch give candy to on Valentine's Day?

-Her sweet-wart!

Why didn't the tree get a Valentine's card?

-Her boyfriend forgot to put a stump on the envelope!

What does a deer wear to a Valentine's dance?

—A buck-cedo!

Knock, knock!
   Who's there?
Will!
   Will who?
Will you be my Valentine?

Why did the boy send a Valentine to a hamburger?

—It was love at first bite!

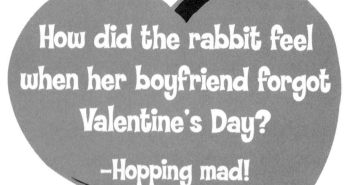

How did the rabbit feel when her boyfriend forgot Valentine's Day?

-Hopping mad!

Knock, knock!
  Who's there?
Bea!
  Bea who?
Bea my Valentine!

Why did the two cats fall in love?

-They were purr-fect for each other!

What did the ghoul write in his Valentine?

-"Tomb it may concern!"

How did the eye doctor sign the love letter to his crush?

—"Your secret adm-eye-rer!"

What did the carton of milk give his girlfriend on February 14th?

—A Valentine's curd!

What are the best kind of flowers to give on Valentine's Day?

—Two-lips!

What do you get when you combine a big dog with a paper heart?

–A Saint Bernard Valentine!

What happened when the Queen of Hearts gave the King of Hearts a Valentine?

–The Joker went wild!

I love you, drummer-you make my heart beat!

I love you, Dracula-you make me batty!

I love you, hair-you grow on me!

I love you, merry-go-round-you make my head spin!

We're breaking up,
canary-you're
so cheep!

We're breaking up,
nose-you smell!

We're breaking up,
skeleton-you're a
lazy bones!

We're breaking up,
bread-you're toast!

How did the cat sign the love letter to her crush?

—"Your secret admire-purr!"

What kind of Valentine's dance do athletes have?

-A basket ball!

Craig: For Valentine's Day I'm drawing a picture of love!

Clizia: Nobody knows what love looks like!

Craig: Now they will!

Fred: What are you writing?

Ned: A Valentine poem that I'm mailing to myself!

Fred: What does it say?

Ned: I won't know until I get the letter!

What kind of flowers does a frog buy on Valentine's Day?

—Croak-uses!

How did the fish sign the love letter to her crush?

—"Your sea-cret admirer!"

What did Frankenstein feel when he met the Bride of Frankenstein?

-Love at first fright!

Boy Chicken: Would you like to go on a date with me?

Girl Chicken: Sure, pick me up at 8 o'cluck!

On what day should you give your best friend flowers?

—Pal-entine's day!

Who plays basketball and makes people fall in love?

—Hoop-id!

What did the hair colorist get on Valentine's Day?

—A dye-mond ring!

What kind of flowers does a butler buy on Valentine's Day?

-Lilies of the Valet!

What does a copy machine like to get on Valentine's Day?

-Cho-collates!

What kind of scissors do you use to make Valentines?

—Pink-ing shears!

Why do people who lie love Valentine's Day?

—Because it's in Fib-ruary!

What did the skunk do when he didn't get any Valentines?

-He caused a stink!

What's in the middle of every Valentine?

—The letter "N"!

What did the ape write on his sweetheart's Valentine?

—"You're the gorilla my dreams!"

What did the chicken give the rooster on Valentine's Day?

—A peck on the cheek!

What game should you play on Valentine's Day?

—Pink pong!

Who did the girl monster give a Valentine to?

—Her boy-fiend!

Why did the apple give the banana a Valentine?

-Because he found her a-peel-ing!

What did the car get on February 14th?

—A Valen-tune up!

I love you, calendar—you make my knees week!

I love you, postage stamp—you send me!

I love you, gymnast—you make my heart flip!

I love you, pole-vaulter—you make my heart leap!

What kind of dance did the pretzel do at the Valentine's Dance?

-The twist!

What did one crybaby give the other crybaby on February 14th?

-A Valen-whine!

What did the pair of pants say at the Valentine's dance?

—"I've got to split!"

What did one flower child say to the other on February 14th?

—"Hippy Valentine's Day!"

What did one Spice give the other Spice on February 14th?

—A Valen-thyme!

What did the dog say to his girlfriend when he took her out to eat for Valentine's Day?

—"Bone appetit!"

What does a green vegetable say on Valentine's Day?

—"Pea Mine!"

What is a butcher's idea of a romantic date?

—Dinner for two by candle-steaks!

What happened when the two caterpillars met?

-It was larva at first sight!

What did the rope give his girlfriend on February 14th?

-A Valentine's cord!

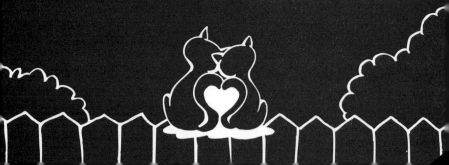

What did Frankenstein do when he got a funny Valentine?

—He laughed his head off!

Who did the grapefruit give candy to on Valentine's Day?

-His sweet-tart!

How did the math teacher sign the love letter to her crush?

−"Your secret add-mirer!"

What did the nerd give his girlfriend for Valentine's Day?

—Dork chocolates!

Why did the girl give her crush a metal Valentine?

—Because she wanted to steel his heart!

What is the beginning of love?

–The letter L!

What does a container of milk hope to get on February 14th?

–A gallon-tine!

What does the alphabet say on Valentine's Day?

—"B Mine!"

What did one grape give the other grape on February 14th?

—A Valen-vine!

How do you say "Happy Valentine's Day" in Italian?

—"Happy Valentine's Day in Italian!"

Which of your fingers likes Valentine's Day the most?

-Your pink-y!

What kind of conversation did the two Valentines have?

—A heart-to-heart talk!

What did one tree say to the other tree on Valentine's Day?

—"I leaf you!"

What did the curtain say to the window on February 14th?

—"Be my valence-tine!"

What flower should you give a new mom?

-Baby's breath!

We're breaking up, robber-you stole my heart!

We're breaking up, peach-you're the pits!

We're breaking up, electric drill-you're bore-ing!

We're breaking up, Tarzan-you're a cheetah!

What does the ocean say on Valentine's Day?

-"Sea Mine!"

What did one basketball player say to the other on February 14th?

—"Hoop-y Valentine's Day!"

What is the end of every relationship?

-The letter P!

What did one ear say to the other ear on Valentine's Day?

—"Nothing will come between us!"

How did the supermarket worker feel when her boyfriend broke up with her on Valentine's Day?

—Broken cart-ed!

What does a locksmith say on Valentine's Day?

—"Key Mine!"

Why is Valentine's Day so great?

—Because it's in Fab-ruary!

Why did the butcher get a lot of dates?

—He was a real beefcake!

What did the coin collector give his girlfriend on Valentine's Day?

-A dime-ond ring!

Why did the twelve roses take a nap?
—Because they kept dozen off!

What did the boy monster call the girl monster who was green and slimy and had long fangs?

—Beautiful!

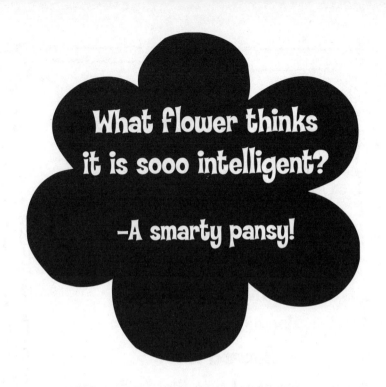

What flower thinks it is sooo intelligent?

-A smarty pansy!

What did the tree get his girlfriend for Valentine's Day?

-A fir coat!

Who did the hotel room go out with on Valentine's Day?

-His suite-heart!

What kind of flower does a writer like to receive on Valentine's Day?

—Proses!

Knock, knock!
  Who's there?
Howard!
  Howard who?
Howard you like to be my Valentine?

What did one mitten say to the other mitten on Valentine's Day?

—"I glove you!"

What's the best day for people to get married?

-Wed-nesday!

Knock, knock!
   Who's there?
Justin!
   Justin who?
Justin time for the Valentine's Day dance!

Where does a werewolf buy his Valentine cards?

—At the Howl-mark store!

How did the girl rabbit send her boyfriend's Valentine?

—By hare mail!

Why did the glove fall in love?

—It was s-mitten!

What does a fork give his girlfriend on February 14th?

-A Valen-tine!

Why did the pilot give the flight attendant a Valentine?

—It was love at first flight!

I love you, joker-you drive me wild!

I love you, lumberjack-you're tree-mendous!

I love you, statue-you're marble-ous!

I love you, magnet-you're so attractive!

We're breaking up, onion-you made me cry!

We're breaking up, convict-you make me jail-ous!

We're breaking up, Civil War soldier-you're revolting!

We're breaking up, trampoline-you make me jumpy!

What do you give a Sorcerer for
Valentine's Day?

—A charm bracelet!

What does a dog hate to hear
on Valentine's Day?

—"Flea Mine!"

Why did the funny Valentine card
change colors?

—It was tickled pink!

What did the booger say to the nose hair on Valentine's Day?

–"I'm stuck on you!"

What did the parsley say to the rosemary?

–"You mean a great dill to me!"

What do you call
a boring date?

-A bland date!

What did one angel say to the other on February 14th?

—"Harp-y Valentine's Day!"

What did one rabbit say to the other on February 14th?

-"Hoppy Valentine's Day!"

What did the sugar cube call his Valentine?

—Sweetie!

What do you call Valentine's candy that was left out in the sun?

—Hot chocolate!

What did the hamburger give the french fries on Valentine's Day?

—An onion ring!

What did the tropical fruit say to her sweetheart when they got married?

-"You are the pineapple of my eye!"

Why didn't the flute give the flooglehorn a Valentine?

  —The flooglehorn was a toot-timer!

Why was the geometry teacher sad about his girlfriend?

  —Because Polly-gone!

What does a golfer say on Valentine's Day?

  -"Tee Mine!"

How did the snowman feel when he got stood up on Valentine's Day?

—Brrr-oken hearted!

What did the bee call his Valentine?

–Honey!

What kind of flowers do stir-fried Vegetables buy on Valentine's Day?

—Pan-sies!

Why didn't the Valentine get any work done?

—Because he was lacey!

Why didn't the statue get a Valentine from his girlfriend?

—She took him for granite!

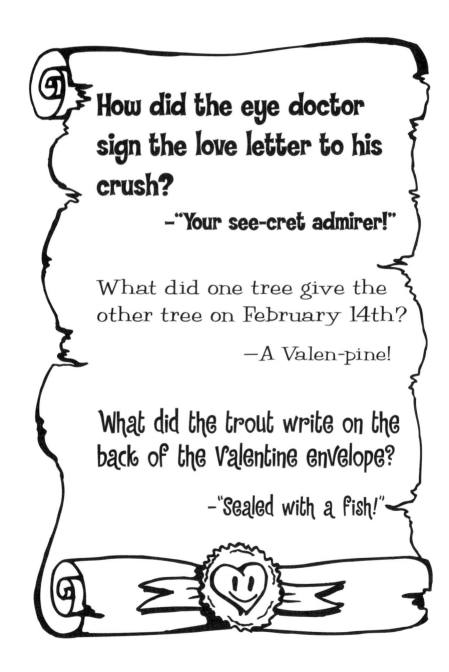

How did the eye doctor sign the love letter to his crush?

-"Your see-cret admirer!"

What did one tree give the other tree on February 14th?

—A Valen-pine!

What did the trout write on the back of the Valentine envelope?

-"Sealed with a fish!"

What kind of flowers does a silly person buy on Valentine's Day?

—Daffy-dills!

Who did the supermarket give candy to on Valentine's Day?

—His sweet-mart!

Where does Swiss cheese buy its Valentine cards?

—At the Hole-mark store!

What did the sorceress write in her Valentine?

—"Best witches!"

What did the jigsaw puzzle say to his Valentine?

-"You complete me!"

What kind of Valentine did the farmer give his wife?

-A corny one!

What did the cow say to his girlfriend on Valentine's Day?

—"Will you moo-rry me?"

Frankenstein: Dracula is dating the Invisible Woman!

Bride of Frankenstein: I don't know what he sees in her!

Why do snowmen love Valentine's Day?

-Because it's in Fe-brrr-uary!

What did one spool of string give the other spool of string on February 14th?

-A Valen-twine!

How did the mallard mend his broken heart?

—He used duck-t tape!

What flowers grow on your face?

—Two-lips!

What kind of gum does an animal lover chew?

-Ba-zoo-ka!

What did the baseball player give his girlfriend for Valentine's Day?

-A big diamond!

What does a pony
use to write a
Valentine card?

—Horse code!

How do you spell Valentine's
Day backwards?

—V-A-L-E-N-T-I-N-E-S-D-A-Y
B-A-C-K-W-A-R-D-S!

What candy do you eat in the schoolyard?

—Recess Pieces!

Why shouldn't you write a Valentine's Day card on an empty stomach?

—It's better to use paper!

Who did the boy with gas give candy to on Valentine's Day?

-His sweet-fart!

What did the ghost give his girlfriend on Valentine's Day?

–A boo-quet of flowers!

What candy bar do dogs hate?

–Kit cat!

What should you eat on Valentine's Day?

—A heart-y meal!

I love you, chimney—you soot me!

Phil: Do you know farts celebrate Valentine's day?

Lil: Yes, they are very scent-imental!

What did one Volcano say to the other on Valentine's Day?

—"I lava you!"

Where do cows like to go on dates?

—To the moo-vies!

What did Dracula give his girlfriend on Valentine's Day?

—A neck-lace!

What's black and white and red all over?

-A zebra holding a stack of valentines!

What did one skeleton give the other skeleton on February 14th?

-A Valen-spine!

Why did the monster dance so badly on his date?

–He had six left feet!

What did the skater give her boyfriend?

–An ice ring!

Why did the Valentine go out with the fish?

—They were heart and sole!

What did the artist tell her boyfriend on Valentine's Day?

-"My art beats for you!"

I love you, geologist—you rock my world!

What did the hippo
say to her Valentine?

—"I love you a ton!"

**I love you, table lamp—
you light up my life!**

What did the hatter say to
Alice?

—"I'm mad about you!"

Why did the perfume bottles get married?

-Because they made perfect scents!

Craig: Did you know the German shepard fell in love with the Chiuaua?

Clizia: Yes, but it was only puppy love!

I love you,
kitty-you're
purr-fect!

I love you,
sailor-let's tie
the knot!

I love you,
mummy-but let's keep
it under wraps!

I love you,
seamstress-you leave
me in stitches!

We're breaking up, computer-our love has crashed!

We're breaking up, doctor-you have no patients!

We're breaking up, cartoonist-you have no character!

We're breaking up, elephant-you are too nosey!

What flowers grow on your tongue?

-Tu-licks!

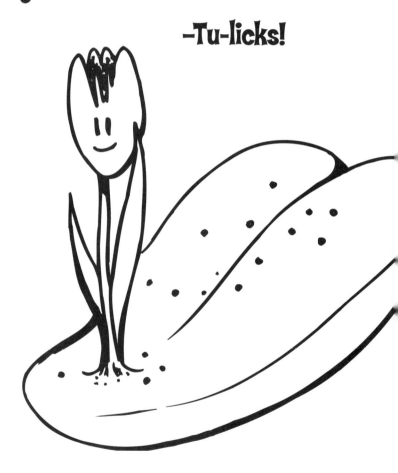

I love you, rug-you floor me!

What flower is dangerous?

—A vio-lent!

I love you, Lancelot-can we go out to-knight?

Where do werewolves go after their wedding?

-On their honey-full-moon!

Why was the prune home alone on Valentine's Day?

—Because it couldn't get a date!

Why did the boy penny ask the girl penny to marry him?

—Because they made perfect cents!

What did one clock give the other clock on February 14th?

–A Valen-time!

How does Dracula ask his girlfriend out to dinner on Valentine's Day?

—"Wanna go for a bite?"

I love you, shoemaker-you touched my sole!

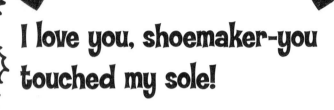

How does a snake sign her Valentine's cards?

—"Love and hisses!"

I love you, gander-you give me goosebumps!

What did one dog say to the other dog after Valentine's Day?

—"We're Rover!"

Craig: Do you know the two birds
fell in love with each other?

Clizia: Yes, they were all
lovey-dovey!

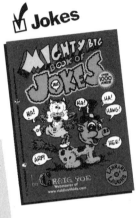